The Last Will

Robert Brustein

A SAMUEL FRENCH ACTING EDITION

SAMUEL FRENCH

FOUNDED 1830

SAMUELFRENCH.COM
SAMUELFRENCH-LONDON.CO.UK

FOR PRODUCTION ENQUIRIES

UNITED STATES AND CANADA
Info@SamuelFrench.com
1-866-598-8449

UNITED KINGDOM AND EUROPE
Plays@SamuelFrench-London.co.uk
020-7255-4302

Each title is subject to availability from Samuel French, depending upon country of performance. Please be aware that *THE LAST WILL* may not be licensed by Samuel French in your territory. Professional and amateur producers should contact the nearest Samuel French office or licensing partner to verify availability.

THE LAST WILL was first produced in Boston by the Commonwealth Shakespeare Company (Artistic Director Steve Maler) and Suffolk University (Arististic Director Marilyn Plotkins) at the Modern Theatre in February 1013. The Boston performance was directed by Steven Maler. The Boston sets were by Eric Levenson, the costumes by Nancy Leary, the lighting by Eric Southern. The Production Manager was Jo Williams and the Stage Manager was Melissa Daroff.

WILLIAM SHAKESPEARE . . . . Allyn Burrows

ANNE HATHAWAY SHAKESPEARE . . . . Brooke Adams

RICHARD BURBAGE. . . . . Jeremiah Kissell

JUDITH SHAKESPEARE . . . . Stacy Fischer

SUSANNA HALL . . . . .Merritt Jansen

FRANCIS COLLINS. . . . . .Billy Meleady

Soon after, it was produced in New York by the Abingdon Theatre (Aristic Director Jan Buttram and Assistant Artistic Director Kim T. Sharp) in April 2013. It was later chosen as two of the entries in China's Wuzhen Festival in May of 2013. The New York production was directed by Austin Pendleton, whose China production was touched up by Jan Buttram. The New York production had sets by Stephen Dobay, costumes by Laura Crow, Lighting by by Travis McHale, and Sound Design by David Margolin Lawson. The production Manager was John Trevellini, and the Production Stage Manager was Mark Hoffner. The New York Cast was as follows:

WILLIAM SHAKESPEARE . . . . Austin Pendleton

ANNE HATHAWAY SHAKESPEARE . . . . Stephanie Roth Haberle

RICHARD BURBAGE. . . . . Jeremiah Kissell

JUDITH SHAKESPEARE . . . . .Christianna Nelson

SUSANNA HALL . . . . .Merritt Jansen

FRANCIS COLLINS. . . . . David Wohl

CHARACTERS

At the beginning of the play, the characters are the following ages:

WILLIAM SHAKESPEARE – 48

ANNE HATHAWAY – 56

SUSANNA SHAKESPEARE (HALL) – 30

JUDITH SHAKESPEARE – 27

FRANCIS COLLINS, LAWYER – 47

RICHARD BURBAGE – 45

SETTING & TIME

The play takes place in the four years between William Shakespeare's return to Stratford in 1612 and his death in 1616 but, since the action is not so much historical as subjective, those four years could take place in four days.

1. Grief fills the room up with my absent child

*(As the lights come up slowly, the shape of a man in grey, ill-fitting clothes can be perceived standing in the doorway of a bedroom. His face is pinched and his hands are seriously gnarled. He is slightly bent. **ANNE HATHAWAY** is in the bed, sleeping fitfully. By slow degrees the darkness lifts, and **ANNE** moves uncomfortably under the covers, half aware of this presence.)*

WILL. Grief fills the room up with my absent child.

*(**ANNE** with a start sits up rigidly.)*

ANNE. Is that you Will? *(long silence while they contemplate each other)* You were not to have been in Stratford until Advent Sunday. Come into the light.

*(**WILL** is moving into the room, blinking hard.)*

ANNE. Why do you lurk in shadow?

WILL. I was watching you sleep. So restless.

ANNE. And you didn't waken me?

WILL. I feared to show my face.

ANNE. Good heavens, why?

WILL. It is a cheerless face.

ANNE. *(peering at him)* You are a lot paler than on your last visit. And your hands. How did they get so gnarled? Are you crippled?

WILL. *(evasive)* It is nothing. The condition will pass.

ANNE. Beware! There is a nasty pestilence in the neighborhood.

WILL. It is even worse in London.

ANNE. It has touched both your brothers.

WILL. Have you seen them?

ANNE. Once, last week. I spoke to Gilbert through the window of his house.

WILL. I spent last evening with him. Face to face.

ANNE. That was madness. God grant that you were not touched.

WILL. I have survived worse plagues. My death will rise not from a pit of pestilence but from a swamp of sores.

ANNE. What does that mean?

WILL. *(ignoring the question)* You said you feared I might grow sick. I am sick. Sick of my life. Its shocks, surprises. Sick of seeing people I love die young.

(an awkward silence)

I have walked a long distance.

ANNE. You didn't ride?

WILL. Part of the way. I felt a need to walk. Barefoot. On sharp stones. I should have crawled. I have come *(pause)* to beg my family's forgiveness for my contemptible behavior as a husband and father.

*(**ANNE** is silent.)*

I have not made you happy.

ANNE. Not often, no.

WILL. I visited you but four weeks a year.

ANNE. And spent your Stratford intervals drinking in the tavern. *(pause)* And ran away to London before the funeral of your only son?

WILL. I saw him in his coffin. That was enough.

ANNE. But to abandon the family just before his burial.

WILL. My Richard was about to open. I was acting in two other plays.

ANNE. You were so invested in your characters that you couldn't say goodbye to your own flesh and blood?

WILL. I said goodbye to Hamnet in my heart, and immortalized his name in a play. Why stay to watch that sad little body being lowered into the indifferent ground.

ANNE. In order to be with your wife and daughters.

WILL. So what you are thinking under that forbearing smile is that my success in the playhouse is nothing to my failure as a husband and a father.

ANNE. I would not have put it that strongly.

WILL. Any other wife would have bashed in my skull with a rusty frying pan.

ANNE. Self-pity is not a manly feature.

WILL. It is an ever present lodger. More at hand than I have ever been to you.

ANNE. You somehow managed to show up for the ceremonial events, like Susanna's marriage.

WILL. Yes, but not, as you say, for the passing of my only son – my impish boy, whose soft moist lips I never kissed goodbye. My sweet young prince, good night. You have entered the silence of your Danish namesake.

ANNE. And how many men have been fortunate enough to install their dead child in the hallowed lists of art.

WILL. You are mocking me, dear Gertrude.

ANNE. My name is Anne.

WILL. I meant to say Anne. My mind misleads from time to time.

ANNE. It is a common failing among those who live by fictions.

WILL. You do mock me, indeed.

ANNE. A little.

WILL. If it is any comfort, I have determined never again to leave your side.

ANNE. And your profession?

WILL. It is over.

ANNE. How can it be over?

WILL. It is over. Do not ask the reasons.

ANNE. And how will we survive?

WILL. I have been acquiring considerable holdings, both here and in the city.

ANNE. So the truant child returns to his home, not as a poor player but as a wealthy landowner?

WILL. Reasonably wealthy. Until a moment ago, I still had a seventh share in the Globe.

(**RICHARD BURBAGE** *enters at this moment, and* **WILL** *turns to speak with him.* **WILL** *for a moment is in another world.*)

BURBAGE. Down to the last rail and floorboard. A stunning catastrophe!

WILL. The entire theatre burned to the ground?

BURBAGE. Predicted by you!

WILL. By me?

BURBAGE. In a characteristic moment of gloom. *(performing)* "The great Globe itself, and all which it inherit, shall dissolve, yea like this insubstantial pageant faded, leave not a rack behind." Very prophetic as things turned out.

WILL. Prospero's great Globe was not only a player's platform, it was also a celestial planet. I was hardly writing about the loss of a playhouse, I was predicting the end of the world.

BURBAGE. That fire ended our world.

(**BURBAGE** *disappears and* **WILL** *turns to* **ANNE** *again.*)

ANNE. You will return to London when your interests, or your appetites, lure you there.

WILL. Believe what you will, my move to Stratford is permanent.

ANNE. Does that mean you intend to resume your marital obligations? Or shall we say, begin them?

WILL. Always the bitter tongue.

ANNE. It is the only tongue God gave me.

WILL. One last question.

ANNE. Yes?

WILL. Over these twenty-four long years of separation, when I was largely an absent imprint on your bed, can you swear, dear Gertrude, that you have always faithfully observed your marriage vows?

ANNE. My name is Anne.

(blackout)

2. And leave not a rack behind

(*ANNE disappears and* **BURBAGE** *reappears with* **WILL** *in a room in his house, handing him a severely burned shepherd's staff.*)

BURBAGE. As actor-manager of the Globe, I brought this souveneir to you. Adam's prop from *As You Like It.*

WILL. But Burbage, how could such sturdy scaffolding be so quickly reduced to cinder and rubble?

BURBAGE. Special effects, man. We were doing *Henry VIII.* The King's first entrance was celebrated by a cannon. The spark touched a thatched roof. The roof sparked the stage. And in less than the length of a brief soliloquy the entire space was a pile of ash and flame.

WILL. And no one was injured?

BURBAGE. Miraculously, not even a groundling, though that buffoon Robert Armin, turned his buttocks towards the blaze as if to extinguish it with noxious gasses. His efforts were rewarded with a huge blister on his arse.

WILL. To risk life and limb for such a barren jape! Was he badly hurt?

BURBAGE. Someone had the wit to douse his flaming breeches with a tankard of ale. But aside from our clown, not a soul among the three thousand spectators suffered serious burns – excepting, of course, the Globe investors, badly scorched by the combustion of their shareholds.

WILL. Myself among them. One clumsy piece of stage business and a major portion of my capital goes up in flames. And on the eve of my *(pause)* retirement.

BURBAGE. You! What about me? My father created that theatre. I was the major shareholder. No need to fear. There's no reason for panic. The company will continue to stage indoor plays at Blackfriars until the

Globe is rebuilt next year. Wait, did you say retirement? We intend to reopen the theatre with a brand new work from you.

WILL. You know I have no intention of writing any more plays.

BURBAGE. I have expressly come to persuade you otherwise. And to tempt you with the news that your fellow players are eager to collect all your dramatic writings into a single folio. Eighteen of your thirty-six plays have never before seen the inside of a printing press.

WILL. Tell the boys to save themselves the paper. Plays are meant to be seen and heard, not read. Only pirates benefit from publication.

BURBAGE. That is precisely the reason for an authorized version – to put an end to all these surreptitious copies, maimed and deformed by counterfeit impostors.

WILL. Who cares?

BURBAGE. Ben Jonson is preparing a Folio of his Works.

WILL. Yes, he thinks by calling them "Works," people won't realize that they are only plays.

BURBAGE. You showed no such qualms when your poems were set in print.

WILL. Poetry is literature. Theatre is the poor stepsister of the arts.

BURBAGE. Now what explains this sudden disdain for the stage after composing the most popular attractions in the language for over two decades?

WILL. *(evasive)* I've lost the will to write.

BURBAGE. No more energy, eh?

WILL. Not a whit.

BURBAGE. Not even for a sonnet?

WILL. Sonnets are like compressed plays. They demand a similar expense of energy.

BURBAGE. Have you run out of ideas? Has the ghost of Christopher Marlowe ceased to whisper in your ear?

WILL. And you, too, spread that idle rumor?

BURBAGE. You must admit your last few plots did seem a little farfetched. *(quoting)* "Jupiter descends in thunder and lightning, sitting on an eagle." Hum! And what about this peculiar stage direction: *"Exit pursued by a bear."* Eagles? Bears? Where are we? In a theatre, or at the Circus Maximus?

WILL. I was experimenting in new forms.

BURBAGE. New forms! Aha! That suggests fresh inspiration. So why such haste to retire? What's the issue? You know you can trust my silence.

WILL. Can I?

BURBAGE. Implicitly.

WILL. All right, though you are hardly famous for your prudence…

BURBAGE. Will!!

WILL. You must swear never to reveal my condition to a living soul, especially my wife.

BURBAGE. I swear. What condition?

WILL. My thoughts have ceased to be consecutive and my eyesight is fading.

BURBAGE. Sheer fatigue. You have been writing too much.

WILL. Is that why I have of late been pulling fistfuls of hair from my scalp? Or why I can no longer grasp a quill in my hand? Look at my fingers – the gnarled claws of a misshapen crab.

BURBAGE. You didn't need a full head of hair to dispatch King Henry to the fields of Agincourt. Or delicate hands to send Orlando to the mat with Charles. Your penmanship was never more than scribbles, anyway. I don't think I ever saw you write your name the same way twice.

WILL. I am never the same man twice.

BURBAGE. But your signature?

WILL. I can barely scratch it out at all now.

BURBAGE. Then dictate your dialogue to an amanuensis. Your verse has always flowed as smoothly as the river Avon.

WILL. That river now is blocked – with decay, debris, and rotten refuse.

BURBAGE. I am very sorry to hear you say that.

WILL. I am the sorry one – a poet whose mind is too muddled to invent coherent iambics. I have grey hairs growing on my brain.

BURBAGE. All right, let's assume you don't write for a spell. How will you pay your rates? Ah, don't you own a parcel of tithes in Stratford?

WILL. Well, half a leasehold interest.

BURBAGE. Then you can support yourself for a term as a provincial landlord, charging extortionate rackrent on your real estate holdings.

WILL. I have too long neglected my family in order to act and write for you at the Globe. I intend to once again assume the responsibilities of a father and a husband.

BURBAGE. And a moneylender.

WILL. *(defiantly)* Yes, and a moneylender.

BURBAGE. Atonement, eh? I guessed you were thinking on your death.

WILL. It crosses my mind from time to time.

BURBAGE. There is talk that your brother, Gilbert, is sinking fast. And that your younger brother Richard is here in a Stratford infirmary suffering from the same disease.

WILL. Yes.

BURBAGE. And your baby brother, Edmund, died of the pestilence in his late twenties. Curious. How explain the way that Shakespeare men attract the black plague. God forbid it should come courting after you.

WILL. I still feel Edmund's loss most keenly.

BURBAGE. I always liked that laddie best. Your brother wasn't much of an actor. He had none of your skills as a writer. But his delicate nature was a rare thing among the King's Men – which may explain why he preferred the company of the King's boys.

WILL. Edmund's sexual preferences were entirely his own business.

BURBAGE. You hardly kept your passion for the Earl of Southampton secret in your sonnets.

WILL. Like most actors, you find it hard to distinguish reality from fiction.

BURBAGE. Like most writers, you find it hard to separate fiction from autobiography.

WILL. Dick, that's a lot of rubbish. Why do actors always think they know more than the playwright about his plays? *(makes as if to leave)*

BURBAGE. *(stopping him)* Calm down, Will, calm down. I've never known you so quick to take offense. Where is the merry reveler of yesteryear?

WILL. Lately, I seem to have lost all my mirth. My spirits hang as heavy as the testicles on an old horse.

BURBAGE. So that explains your return to Stratford, eh? Where every third thought shall be your grave?

WILL. I don't have three consecutive thoughts. I am sick, nursing slow poison in my veins.

BURBAGE. Not from the pestilence!!

WILL. No, from Emilia Lanier.

BURBAGE. That affair ended years ago. What has your dark lady left you other than regrets?

WILL. A lethal legacy whose progress is plodding but persistent.

BURBAGE. After twenty years?

WILL. Twenty years is the life of the disease. The canker likes to make its final passage through the brain.

BURBAGE. *(taken aback)* You'll soon recover your faculties.

WILL. You think so? Already my mind is affected.

BURBAGE. How so?

WILL. I who was known for mercy and forgiveness have now turned sour and suspicious. But, much much worse for a writer, I am finding it harder to tell fiction from fact.

BURBAGE. And the cause?

WILL. Either the pox my mistress gave me or the mercury my doctors dosed me with to kill it.

BURBAGE. My poor old friend, you have been suffering.

WILL. Please tell no one. I am hoping rest will cure this affliction.

BURBAGE. Well, talk won't cure it. Let's drown it out! I'm told you have a particularly agreeable tavern in the outskirts.

WILL. You mean The Cage?

BURBAGE. The Cage. A well-named playpen for a thirsty animal.

WILL. The lodgings there are good as well.

BURBAGE. Then the Cage is where I'll lay my head this night.

WILL. And I will pay a call on brother Gilbert – perhaps my last before he dies.

BURBAGE. And here's another vow I'll make. Until you decide to return to London, each year at Whitsuntide I'll reenter the bars of the Cage to join you for a bibulous reunion.

WILL. *(somewhat dazed)* Agreed.

BURBAGE. Is the establishment worth our custom?

WILL. It's not the Boar's Head or the Mermaid, but the Madeira is imported directly from the sugar fields of Portugal.

BURBAGE. Madeira wine it is then, man. After one or two bottles of that divine ambrosia, I warrant, you'll have your head down the bodice of some busty barmaid, warbling "Where the bee sucks there suck I."

WILL. Provided I have the breath to sing the song or the memory to recall the lyric.

BURBAGE. Or the hunger to suck the bosom.

    *(**WILL** walks unsteadily ahead and collapses. **BURBAGE** goes to his aid.)*

Will! Will! Are you all right?

    *(**WILL** comes slowly to his senses. **BURBAGE** helps him up.)*

3. Incestuous sheets

(We are back in **ANNE**'s *bedroom)*

WILL. Gertrude, wake up! Is it true?

ANNE. Stop this Gertrude nonsense! I am your wife, not your Hamlet's mother.

WILL. Is it true?

ANNE. Is what true?

WILL. Who is here with you? There! Hiding in your closet!

ANNE. Who would be there?

WILL. The adulterous brother. Dead for a ducat.

ANNE. Will, you're frightening me. Where have you come from?

WILL. From my brother Gilbert's bedside. He will not live another week.

ANNE. Is he suffering?

WILL. Horribly. Fearful gripes in his bowels. Spastic aches in his joints.

ANNE. I am told he was moved to the infirmary at St. Anne's.

WILL. You mean the charnel house at St. Anne's. That is where I found his carcass, half-alive amidst a dozen decomposing corpses.

ANNE. I grieve to hear you say it.

WILL. I do not doubt you grieve to hear me say it. I came home to ask for your forgiveness. Now you must ask for mine.

ANNE. What does that mean?

*(***WILL*** is silent.)*

WILL. I say I visited my brother.

ANNE. You should not have exposed yourself to the hazards of the black death.

WILL. What I cannot endure is blacker death that's called betrayal. But one month gone.

ANNE. You talk in riddles.

WILL. *(ignoring the question)* When did you visit Gilbert last?

ANNE. Before he was taken to St. Anne's. I feared contamination.

WILL. Your contamination was the subject of my visit.

ANNE. He mentioned me?

WILL. In a manner of speaking. He wished to make confession.

ANNE. What kind of confession?

WILL. A confession that he always loved you, that his love for you was hairy with lust.

ANNE. He would not say so.

WILL. No, he did not say so. He could not speak. His mouth was swollen with pustules. But his eyes...his every gasp confirmed his passion for you. Is it true?

ANNE. *(firmly)* No.

WILL. He never consummated the act of darkness with you?

ANNE. Never!

WILL. *(passionately)* Then why was he clutching your handkerchief?

ANNE. Which handkerchief?

WILL. This one! *(removing a fraying handkerchief from his tunic, which bears the initials AS)* He spewed his bloody rheum on it.

ANNE. (ANNE *recoils from the handkerchief.)* If that thing is mine, he never got it from me.

WILL. Of course it's yours – the gift I gave you at our nuptials.

ANNE. I haven't seen that thing in years.

WILL. Then how did it come into my brother's hand?

ANNE. That you must tell me.

WILL. It was Gilbert I left to care for you, when first I went to tour the provinces.

ANNE. You left me with a boy twelve years my junior.

WILL. And I was a boy eight years your junior. Which did not prevent you from luring me into that rye field...

ANNE. It was a corn field.

WILL. …for a late summer tumble, followed by an unwanted pregnancy and an over-hasty marriage. Where did you lure Gilbert?

ANNE. Are you suggesting I seduced that boy?

WILL. Yes, and he sired the twins, born three years later, after I had joined the acting company in Leamington?

ANNE. Nine months after.

WILL. Ten months after.

ANNE. Nine and a half. I was late. What does that prove?

WILL. That you had lain with Gilbert one month after my departure. I never thought of it before, but now that handkerchief gives it proof. Most wicked speed to post with such dexterity to incestuous sheets.

ANNE. I never laid with him.

WILL. Then who was the father?

ANNE. Who else but you, you demented poet!

WILL. And will you swear that you have never known another's body in all the twenty-seven years since first I left for London?

ANNE. Can you swear the same?

WILL. That was not my question.

ANNE. I have been a true and loyal spouse.

WILL. Of course you would plead innocence. It is the common litany of the faithless wife. But why should I believe it?

ANNE. Calm yourself!

(BURBAGE *is seen at this moment, in* WILL*'s imagination, speaking a speech from* Othello.)

BURBAGE. Nay, but to live
In the rank sweat of an enseamed bed,
Stew'd in corruption, honeying and making love
Over the nasty sty…to make me
The fixed finger for the time of scorn
To point his slow and moving finger at….

ANNE. Adultery? Incest?

WILL. Aye, all the offenses I oft foretold, though I mistook the miscreant. My brothers Richard and Edmund were guiltless of the depravity I assigned their namesakes – the murderous Richard, the deceitful Edmund. *(hitting his forehead)* Fool! Fool! It was my nearest brother Gilbert who proved the Claudius of this bedroom drama, stalking my wife with ravishing strides.

ANNE. I deny this slander, William Shakespeare. You are a husband who has returned home but twice a twelvemonth, and then for less than two weeks visit. For twenty-seven years, I have endured our separation without protest or complaint. For twenty-seven years, I have suffered a marriage without affection or endearment. And now I must suffer insults, too?

WILL. Shameless harlot!

ANNE. And where is the evidence for this loathsome charge? Your brother's eyes!

WILL. Give me some living proof.

ANNE. No woman can offer proof of innocence. Only of guilt. My fidelity you must take on faith.

(silence)

(BURBAGE *is seen again, this time as Leontes in* The Winter's Tale.*)*

BURBAGE. Too hot, too hot!

WILL. Too hot, too hot!

BURBAGE. But to be paddling palms and pinching fingers,
As now they are, and making practiced smiles
As in a looking glass…oh, that is entertainment,
My bosom likes not, nor my brows. Mamillius,
Art thou my boy?

(back to **WILL** *and* **ANNE***)*

WILL. Hamnet, art thou my boy?

ANNE. How can you doubt it?

WILL. A woman's reputation is like the air it is made of.

ANNE. I have been both mother and father to my abandoned children. I have kept their minds pure and, except for our poor Hamnet, their bodies sound.

WILL. But you cannot swear that Hamnet and Judith were truly of my loins.

ANNE. *(impatient)* I will listen no more.

(She makes as if to leave. WILL *throws her back on the bed.)*

WILL. Come and sit you down. You will not leave here till I set you up a glass where you will see the inmost part of you, and admit your infidelity.

ANNE. I deny your charges fully.

WILL. Gilbert is preparing to meet his God, suspended between delirium and death. Why would he lie?

ANNE. I grieve for Gilbert, but he had as much appeal for me as your dead brother, Edmund, and you know where his preferences lay.

*(*WILL *sits on the bed.* ANNE*'s eyes follow him quizzically.)*

WILL. You would charge my youngest brother with sodomy rather than admit your adultery with Gilbert.

ANNE. You would deny your brother's unmanliness, yet believe false whispers about your wife's fidelity.

WILL. This is not the first I have heard of your transgressions.

ANNE. And what about your own? All England knows of your affair with that whore Lanier.

WILL. Admit your infidelity!

ANNE. I admit nothing!

WILL. *(pause, to the audience – and himself – darkly)* I must change my will.

(blackout)

4. Let's kill all the lawyers

(**WILL** *walks into a scene with his new lawyer,* **FRANCIS COLLINS.**)

WILL. Thank you for seeing me, Lawyer Collins.

COLLINS. A rare privilege, Master Shakespeare.

WILL. I am a gentleman now, Lawyer Collins. I have realized my father's lifelong ambition to own a family crest. I would have my coat of arms imprinted on all our future documents and myself referred to in legal papers as William Shakespeare, Gent.

COLLINS. I am happy to oblige you, William Shakespeare, er, Gent. You have accumulated many well-earned honors since last we met. I still think of us as fellow schoolboys,

WILL. A lot of time has passed since last we wrestled with our Latin ablatives, Lawyer Collins.

COLLINS. Indeed it has, indeed it has.

WILL. Your professional practice goes well?

COLLINS. Thanks be to God, the people of Stratford upon Avon are still extremely litigious.

WILL. A vice of age. I share it. Well, to the business. My old lawyer having died under me like a horse with the spavins, I am in need of a new mount. My elder daughter, Susanna, has spoken of her high regard for you.

COLLINS. I am flattered to have her endorsement and eager to offer my equestrian services, sir. There was a time when you were not so happily disposed towards the legal herd.

WILL. *(puzzled)* Yes?

COLLINS. *(quoting from 2* Henry VI*)* "The first thing we do, let's kill all the lawyers."

WILL. I am flattered to find you so familiar with my chronicles. But those sentiments were spoken by an illiterate ruffian whose name has momentarily dropped from memory.

COLLINS. Dick the Butcher to the rebel Jack Cade.

WILL. That one. You may remember that this rogue Cade also wanted to hang a lord for erecting a grammar school.

COLLINS. Not a few schoolboys have harbored similar ambitions.

WILL. Indeed, indeed. But to the point, Lawyer Collins, I need a new will. Certain facts have recently surfaced that compel substantial changes in my bequests.

COLLINS. That can be accomplished.

WILL. Without exorbitant increases in the fees, I trust. I have already wasted a king's ransom preparing this damnable document, not to mention months of precious time.

COLLINS. I think I can save on time, if it prove not a complicated indenture. May I see the old will? *(He examines it.)* Are the amendments to be many? The simpler the adjustments, the lower the costs.

WILL. They will largely affect my wife's portion of the inheritance. And, to a lesser degree, that of my two surviving children. I have not yet determined how.

COLLINS. You would want to provide more for your eldest daughter, Susanna, I assume. She is underrepresented in this document.

WILL. And for Judith.

COLLINS. *(looking over documents)* Your wife, Anne Shakespeare, née Hathaway, is now scheduled to inherit, as her dower's portion, your Stratford residence, New Place, so long as she shall live, in addition to one third of your existing tithes and rentals as well as all new lands acquired from now until your death.

WILL. Strike all that out!

COLLINS. What?

WILL. Expunge everything in the will that pertains to that deceitful woman. She is not to receive the slightest portion of my holdings.

COLLINS. Nothing?

WILL. Not a square foot of earth.

COLLINS. That will be scanned. You and she have been man and wife for – what?

WILL. I don't know. Decades.

COLLINS. Well, she enjoys, as a result, certain inalienable rights, as for example, a portion of your estate during her lifetime, including the house she lives in. Legally, you cannot leave her disinherited, penniless, without a stone to rest her head on.

WILL. Oh, I'll give her something hard to rest her head on. Our nuptial couch. That iron bed is petrified with age and stiffened with sin.

COLLINS. May I be allowed to speak…?

WILL. Succinctly, please. You are being paid by the hour.

COLLINS. What terrible event has transpired between you to warrant such drastic action?

WILL. The usual trifling nothings that trouble a modern marriage – adultery, cuckoldry, incest.

COLLINS. Do you know these things for certain?

WILL. I know my wife for certain. And I have learned "these things" from an unimpeachable source.

COLLINS. I assume you have thought deliberately about this settlement. It should not be undertaken lightly, though I agree with your decision to provide a substance for Susanna.

WILL. And don't forget Judith.

(**JUDITH** *is seen on stage, talking with* **BURBAGE,** *while* **COLLINS** *mouths words without being heard.*)

JUDITH. You are the one person whose advice he trusts. That is why I'm asking you to plead on my behalf…

BURBAGE. Judith, you shall have your Quiney, if I have any influence in the matter. Have no fear. I will make him think the idea his own.

(**WILL** *shakes his head to clear it, then returns to his scene with* **COLLINS**)

COLLINS. Master Shakespeare, did you hear me?

WILL. What did you say?

COLLINS. That if you decide to change your mind…

WILL. I am firm. I have sworn. My wife gets no more than the minimum the law requires.

COLLINS. Then I suggest five men to witness your signature. That should be enough to satisfy any city authority who might inquire after the reason for your changes. We do not need questions spread throughout the village about your marriage.

WILL. We'll invent some story. After all, I am a fabulist.

COLLINS. Think a little more upon it. And then let us talk again in a week.

WILL. Sooner, if you please. My last will took over two years and twenty-five guineas to complete. I want this one finished quickly. If you haven't recorded the revisions within a week I may be forced to look to other legal stables.

COLLINS. I can promise to finish the process in a week, but no sooner. Unlike four-legged animals, lawyers are obliged to maintain a reasonable pace.

WILL. Not too leisurely a pace, understand? Or else, we won't kill all the lawyers, eh? We'll just geld them. *(He laughs.)*

5. Which of you doth love us most

(**BURBAGE** *in conversation with* **JUDITH** *at The Cage.* **WILL** *hears* **JUDITH** *laughing and leaves* **COLLINS** *to join them.*)

BURBAGE. I have just been having the most engaging conversation with your daughter.

WILL. Have you now? How are you, sweet Judith? Are you well?

JUDITH. Very well. And you, dear Father?

WILL. Happy to find you well.

(He takes her in his arms.)

BURBAGE. I haven't seen this charming creature now for, what is it, ten or fifteen years? She has grown into a most appealing young lady.

WILL. Beware of Burbage, Judith. He gargles with rose water and brushes his teeth with love potions. He is notorious for breaking hearts.

JUDITH. He has often broken mine upon the stage. But, alas, it is promised to another.

WILL. *(Sternly)* Indeed, daughter. Is a father permitted to know the identity of this fortunate man?

JUDITH. I intended to tell you, the moment he and I agreed to join our hands.

WILL. And the name of the happy suitor is…?

JUDITH. Thomas Quiney.

WILL. The tobacconist Quiney?

JUDITH. He is also now a vintner. He recently bought The Cage here, your favorite tavern.

BURBAGE. Aha, that augurs a future of excellent Madeira at affordable prices.

WILL. So that's why I find you in a tavern. If I am not mistaken, Thomas Quiney is somewhat younger than you are, no?

JUDITH. I am twenty-eight. He is twenty-four.

BURBAGE. Not too many years ago, as legend tells us, a Stratford woman of twenty-six married a local boy of eighteen.

WILL. Precisely my point.

JUDITH. Father, Thomas and I are very much in love. Give us your blessing. I am somewhat older than he is, true, but in every other way we are well-matched.

WILL. Thomas Quiney. Thomas Quiney. I seem to remember some other impropriety associated with that name.

JUDITH. *(hesitantly)* You are alluding to his previous romance with Margaret Wheeler.

WILL. Yes. Why did he not marry this Wheeler woman?

JUDITH. She died.

WILL. The cause?

JUDITH. She lost her life in childbirth.

WILL. And the child?

JUDITH. Stillborn.

WILL. And without benefit of clergy, I assume. How did the lad avoid being dragged before the Bawdy Court?

JUDITH. He *was* brought there and, after confessing to carnal copulation, was charged with whoredom and uncleanness.

BURBAGE. The customary state of man.

WILL. *(ignoring him)* And the punishment?

JUDITH. He was ordered to do open penance before the congregation in a white sheet for three consecutive Sundays.

WILL. I am sorry to have missed such a spectacle.

JUDITH. They remitted that part of the sentence in return for a five shilling fine.

WILL. And this five-shilling whoremonger in the white sheet aspires to become the son-in-law of William Shakespeare, Gent.?

BURBAGE. Are we forgetting another Stratford woman whose stomach was stretched without benefit of clergy?

JUDITH. If I can forgive him, Father, then you can, too.

BURBAGE. Of course he can.

WILL. I married your mother to legitimize your sister, Susanna. Not like this Quiney knave who let a woman die unshriven with no hope of salvation.

BURBAGE. Will, yours has always been the largest and warmest heart amongst us. Why has it grown so hard?

WILL. *(after a pause)* Of my two daughters you have been the younger and the nearer joy. I had hoped to spend my fading years in your sweet company, to have you by my bed to ease my final breaths. But your insistence on this mismatched marriage gives me pause. *(Losing it)* To be frank, I have lately been nursing doubts about your parentage…

JUDITH. Father!

BURBAGE. My dear Will…

WILL. Peace, Burbage. Come not between the dragon and his wrath.

BURBAGE. If you must quote from your own plays, Will, borrow wiser characters. Lear was a foolish old man.

WILL. Dick, stay out of family affairs.

BURBAGE. "To plainness honors' bound when good friends fall to folly," as Kent told Lear. I remember your characters better than you do. After all, I originated most of them.

WILL. You have been my friend and collaborator for many years. But this is not a play. It is a private matter. Do not meddle in things that don't concern you.

BURBAGE. I am your considerate stone. We'll talk again when you are in a calmer mood. Should I be needed in the next few days, you'll find me here at The Cage awaiting your company with a glass of Quiney's excellent Madeira. Judith, I have not given up yet.

(He leaves. Enter **SUSANNA HALL,** *née* **SHAKESPEARE.** *She is only 31 and very voluptuous, though already beginning to turn a bit matronly.)*

SUSANNA. Dear father, I thought I'd find you here.

WILL. Well met, Susanna, you come in time to see your sister, Cordelia, being written out of my will.

SUSANNA. Cordelia?

WILL. Judith. *(hitting the side of his head)* Judith, Judith, Judith.

SUSANNA. What has Judith done to provoke such impetuous action, dear my father. I hope I am not in danger of receiving such wrath.

WILL. You have been a loving and legitimate daughter. There will be no like changes in your patrimony.

JUDITH. If you are suggesting I was illegitimate, then so was my dead twin Hamnet.

WILL. Peace. No more.

SUSANNA. You speak of your will, dear father. I trust you are not thinking on your death. You are too deeply loved to entertain such thoughts.

WILL. Every man thinks upon his death, Susanna. Some men think of nothing else. But how are you, girl? And your husband and my grand-daughter?

SUSANNA. Doctor Hall is well, but weary. All his waking hours are occupied with treating victims of the pestilence, and protecting young Elizabeth from infection. *(nodding to* **JUDITH***)* Judith, I have neglected to greet you. I hope you are well.

JUDITH. You see how well I am, sister. And you, are you and your husband still pursuing sinners with the Anabaptists?

SUSANNA. John and I are moderate in our religious beliefs.

JUDITH. Ah, so that's why he's informing on Catholic recusants.

SUSANNA. Ever the plaindealer with the razor tongue, my dearest sister.

JUDITH. Ever the zealot with the forkéd tongue, my dearest
    sister.

WILL. I see your affection for each other remains as strong
    as ever. I wonder if, when I am absent, you express a
    similar tenderness for me.

SUSANNA. Put me to the test, dear parent, and you shall
    find my love so great it cannot be expressed except in
    your incomparable verse.

WILL. And you, dear daughter?

JUDITH. I do not wear my heart upon my sleeve, dear
    father. I lack the rubbery glib of the lips prescribed for
    flattery. I wonder that a man so sensitive to language
    would not be better able to detect dissembling.

WILL. And that is all you have to say to me?

JUDITH. Father, my family duties are divided,

I owe you for my life and education…

But I would have Tom Quiney as my husband,

And just as my mother elected you before her father,

So I must choose my husband, if you approve or not.

WILL. Then let him beware, Desdemona. You have deceived
    your father and may deceive him.

JUDITH. Your loving daughter, Judith.

WILL. What?

JUDITH. My name is Judith, your legitimate daughter, a
    lawful member of an honorable family. And in order to
    perpetuate that line, Shakespeare will be the Christian
    name of our first-born son.

SUSANNA. Shrewd move.

JUDITH. Not shrewd, but practical, for the survival of our
    name.

WILL. Hush, Susanna. Judith touches a tender chord. After
    Hamnet died, I thought the Shakespeare name would
    die with me.

JUDITH. In return, I ask the right to marry whom I please.

WILL. No. I like the wholesome cheer of Shakespeare. I do
    not like the tiny whine of Quiney.

JUDITH. His surname shall be Quiney or he'll have an altogether different Christian name.

SUSANNA. How about Shakespeare Hall? Should we present our daughter with a younger brother, John and I would feel most privileged to name him for his celebrated grandfather.

WILL. Shakespeare Hall? Shakespeare Hall? Sounds like a Grammar School refectory. Judith, your stubbornness shall not go unpunished. A pity. I loved you most.

(**WILL** *enters a scene with* **COLLINS.**)

COLLINS. *(carrying a sheaf of papers)* Now let me understand you. – You wish to disinherit your wife, Anne, and reduce the inheritance of your younger daughter, Judith, if she marries Thomas Quiney, while giving the major portion of your estate to your elder daughter, Susanna Hall. I will not inquire into the reasons for these actions. I simply want to be precise about the bequests.

WILL. What are those papers?

COLLINS. Your first will.

WILL. Read it. We'll make the changes as we proceed.

COLLINS. Very well.

(back with **JUDITH***)*

JUDITH. Father…

WILL. Hence, and avoid my sight.

6. I am not in my perfect mind

COLLINS. *(reading)* "In the name of God amen I William Shackspeare"…*Shackspeare?*?

WILL. Go on.

COLLINS. "Vincesimo Quinto die/JanuariI MartiI Anno Regni/DominI nostrI JacobI nunc/Regis Angliae et decimo/ Testamentum/ WillemI Shackspeare/ Registreur"

WILL. You're reading my will?

COLLINS. The preamble.

WILL. *(breaking in)* The Latin, I assume, was required to help justify my former lawyer's excessive legal fees.

COLLINS. It is required.

WILL. Very well, continue.

COLLINS. "I William Shackspeare of Stratford Upon Avon in perfect health and memory God be praised do make and ordain this my last will and testament in manner and form following. That is to say first I commend my soul into the hands of God my creator hoping and assuredly believing through Jesus Christ to partake of life everlasting. And my body to the earth whereof it is made."

WILL. Who composed these pious platitudes?

COLLINS. Your old attorney, based on customary convention.

WILL. It's not a will, it's a funeral oration. My God, I'm supposed to be a poet. Who would believe such sanctimonious patter was ever composed by me?

COLLINS. We can work on the language after we make our alterations.

WILL. Yes, the alterations are the heart of the matter.

COLLINS. You want to leave Judith with a modest sum of money…

WILL. …on the strict provision that she does not marry Thomas Quiney.

COLLINS. Here is how I have framed the new bequest. *(reading)* "And so I devise and bequeath the said Hundred and Fifty Pounds to be set out by my executors and overseers for the best benefit of her and her issue..." Do I have the sum correct?

WILL. It is correct.

COLLINS. ...not to be paid unto her so long as she shall be married but my will is that she shall have the consideration yearly paid unto her during her life and after her decease the said stock...

WILL. This is Greek to the other's Latin. Where do you lawyers learn to generate this gibberish? Write that she will be penalized if she marries.

COLLINS. I will revise it in clearer language, I promise. Let us consider Susanna.

WILL. Susanna shall be the executor of my estate and have the largest share.

COLLINS. That, I understand, would include the two tenements on the grounds, all of your barns, stables, orchards, gardens taken within the towns, hamlets, villages and fields of Stratford upon Avon, chattels, leases, jewels, and household stuff, all of your plate...

WILL. Except my silver and gilt bowl, which shall go to Judith. *(softening in the memory)* We used to sail paper boats in it when she was still a child.

COLLINS. And Susanna is to inherit New Place.

WILL. Yes. Yes. In partnership with her physician husband, John Hall, who will supervise my passage unto the grave.

COLLINS. If I may suggest...

WILL. Yes?

COLLINS. I would advise removing her husband from the will.

WILL. For what purpose.?

COLLINS. Pure caution. One can never predict the future course of a marriage.

WILL. That is most certain.

COLLINS. Any other legatees?

WILL. I have nothing but tears to leave the dead child, Hamnet. But I do want to bequeath a token to his namesake, my neighbor Hamnet Sadler. Twenty-six shillings eight pence for the purchase of a ring. And twenty six shillings eight pence each to my fellow players, John Heminge, Henry Condell, and Richard Burbage, also to buy them rings.

COLLINS. *(writing)* Charities? Hospices?

WILL. Yes, yes, of course. Ten pounds to the poor of Stratford.

COLLINS. Most generous. *(writes)* And finally your wife, Anne. Am I to understand she gets nothing beyond her dower rights?

WILL. Not true. She gets my second best bed.

COLLINS. *(making a note)* Ah yes, your second best bed.

WILL. Better than she deserves.

COLLINS. And who will receive your very best bed?

WILL. I have decided to be buried with it. It will be my funeral pyre.

COLLINS. One last question. How would you like your surname spelled? I have counted twenty variations on it including Shagspere and Shackespere. It is "Shackspeare" in your first will.

WILL. I have no strong feelings either way.

COLLINS. Not even about your name!!? **(SHAKESPEARE** *is silent.)* This could be questioned, as evidence of an unsound mind. *(more silence)* I assume that you can provide a wholesome answer to any of these questions?

WILL. *(in another world)* Make you a wholesome answer? I cannot. My wit's diseased. But sir, such answer as I can make, you shall command.

COLLINS. *(taken aback)* Yes. All right. I will finish drawing up the new will presently, and bring it up for signature before five witnesses.

WILL. Do it swiftly, whilst my mind remains stable and my fingers still able to hold a quill.

(blackout)

7. If not I'll ne'er trust medicine

*(As the last part of this scene is taking place, **COLLINS** is walking into a scene with **SUSANNA**.)*

SUSANNA. Has he signed it yet?

COLLINS. The will is signed, making you his primary beneficiary.

SUSANNA. (**SUSANNA** *throws her arms around him in a passionate embrace.*) Oh, the difference of man and man!

COLLINS. But signed with the greatest difficulty. The autograph is almost illegible. From the look of his fingers he will never again put his name to another document.

SUSANNA. At least, not another will.

COLLINS. Indeed.

SUSANNA. Or write another play, I hope.

COLLINS. You do not like his writings?

SUSANNA. I do not like the stage.

COLLINS. You must have liked *Othello.* How else would you have had the wit to put your mother's handkerchief into Gilbert's dying grasp?

SUSANNA. I am my father's daughter. And I saw a few of his plays before I joined my husband's Puritan cause.

COLLINS. And obviously profited from them.

SUSANNA. No, for what has his profession brought our family, but endless separations, drunken debauches, and rowdy companions?

COLLINS. It has brought you the main substance of his will.

SUSANNA. His ill-gotten gains.

COLLINS. And this from the eldest child of the greatest dramatic poet in the land.

SUSANNA. According to my pastor, this greatest dramatic poet in the land is a heretic. At first, to write like a Papist, conjuring up ghosts and goblins. And then to declare that Roman gods control the destiny of men. And then, to spit out godless rubbish about the primacy of nature.

COLLINS. Neither you nor your Church should criticize the writing of William Shakespeare. He has lost his good nature. His mind is dark and cloudy. He is easily provoked. But his poetry is sublime.

SUSANNA. I was not taught to read his plays, nor anything else, for that matter. But my visits to his theatre have exposed me to little more than idolatry and wantonness. You may be certain that our religious party, once it seizes power, will lock up those playhouses as abominations unto the Lord.

COLLINS. I fear that your religious party will lock up more than our playhouses. They will seal up our bedchambers, too. Do not the Anabaptists also consider a relationship like ours an abomination unto the Lord?

SUSANNA. I doubt it not. That is why it must be kept a secret.

COLLINS. How can you embrace a sect that once accused you falsely of adulterous behavior?

SUSANNA. It was not my Church that did so, it was that libel-monger, John Lane.

COLLINS. And thanks in no small part to my legal skills, your Church excommunicated the miscreant for bearing false witness. I am still awaiting my fee for that labor of love.

SUSANNA. You have already received an ample retainer, but here is one more installment. *(a prolonged kiss)* In the eyes of my Lord, you are my true husband. My sanctuary lies in your strong arms. *(**COLLINS** goes to kiss her again, but she turns away.)* But let us concentrate on the matter at hand. The amended document will be proof against all question?

COLLINS. I have brought it to probate with five witnesses to the signature.

SUSANNA. Why so many?

COLLINS. So it will never be contested.

SUSANNA. Not even if he changes his mind and writes another will?

COLLINS. There will be no other will.

SUSANNA. How can you be so sure?

COLLINS. The state of his decaying brain. The condition of his twisted hands. The vigilance of his legal counsel.

SUSANNA. And if he recovers?

COLLINS. Then he will dictate his amendments to me, as his lawyer, who will dutifully deposit them into the legal section of the refuse bin.

SUSANNA. And, if all else fails, there are always medicines.

COLLINS. Medicines?

SUSANNA. They have been known to kill as well as cure.

COLLINS. I will act as if I hadn't heard that.

SUSANNA. Once my father is in hellfire and my husband back in Scotland, where he belongs, we will have the means to enjoy our love in comfort for all eternity. Is that not sufficient payment?

COLLINS. Yes, so long as you promise to will your body to me for all eternity.

SUSANNA. *(sliding into his arms)* On that piece of property, you already have a sizeable equity, repaid in nightly increments. Soon you will own it in perpetuity. *(They embrace.)*

8. A poor bare forked animal

(**SHAKESPEARE** *and* **BURBAGE** *at The Cage. Both are a little drunk.*)

BURBAGE. Will, listen to me. Even if your suspicions should prove justified…

WILL. Suspicions!

BURBAGE. Where is your power of forgiveness?

WILL. How does one forgive betrayals of such magnitude?

BURBAGE. You have no proof that your wife betrayed you. To me, it all adds up to much ado about a handkerchief.

WILL. What would you have me do? Behold her topped?

BURBAGE. Who first said that? Your demi-devil Iago. If Othello had been more mistrustful of false rumors, he never would have smothered an innocent woman.

WILL. My brother, Gilbert, was no Iago. He was an honest, plainspoken man.

BURBAGE. So everyone thought Iago. And what about your daughter Judith? Why pour your wrath on her?

WILL. I have not eliminated her from my will. I have simply made the size of her inheritance dependent on her choice of husband.

BURBAGE. And left the major part of your estate to Susanna.

WILL. She, at least, I know to be a true child of my loins.

BURBAGE. As Goneril was to Lear. Enough of this, let's drink.

(*They do so, in silence.*)

I hear today you carried out your first foreclosure. Really? Who?

WILL. A tenant farmer named Chapman.

BURBAGE. He failed to pay his rent?

WILL. Three of his workers fell ill with the plague. His wife as well.

BURBAGE. So give him time to till his land again, man.

WILL. That was my instinct. But he set up such a roar about my miserly character and his shuttered property that we nearly came to blows.

BURBAGE. This man is penniless. Show him some compassion, Will.

WILL. And if I yield to this compassion how will I recover my losses from the Globe? Anyway, it is only a partial eviction. He can stay in the house for a few months while my other tenants work his enclosure.

BURBAGE. You say you are confusing reality with your writing. It is time for you to learn wisdom from your own plays.

WILL. Which plays?

BURBAGE. *(quoting)* "Take physic pomp/Expose thyself to feel what wretches feel/That thou mayst shake the superflux to them/And show the heavens more just."

WILL. I wrote that?

BURBAGE. It's from *King Lear.*

WILL. Lear wasn't a landlord.

BURBAGE. You feel no pity for this farmer.

WILL. The stars, I fear, will continue on their unjust course, however I behave. And at present I am in no financial condition to shake a superflux. Yes, I must confess I felt some qualms about the old fellow, standing all ashiver in the pelting rain.

BURBAGE. Poor Tom's acold.

WILL. "Off, off, you lendings. Unaccommodated man is no more but such a poor, bare, forked animal." See, I do occasionally remember my own dialogue. *(JUDITH enters.)* What, you still in this tavern?

JUDITH. I help out Quiney in the taproom.

WILL. A barmaid now, too. Better for you to stay at home and tend your mother.

JUDITH. She needs no help from me, father. She is most in need of you. I have never known her so despondent.

WILL. She misses your Uncle Claudius.

BURBAGE. Gilbert.

JUDITH. No, sir, she misses you.

WILL. I doubt that. She has had company enough.

JUDITH. It is not my mother you should be tarring with charges of adultery, but your daughter, Susanna. Were you aware that during your absence a certain John Lane accused her of being "naught" with a neighbor. He also accused her of contracting the clap.

WILL. I had heard of this case. It was a malicious slander. She was exonerated. Your mother would not pass the same test.

JUDITH. Forgive my frankness, father, but you are hardly the best judge of my mother's character. You are not the loving man you were when last you left here. You are no longer rendering balanced judgments. And now, I could not help but hear, you have evicted Miles Chapman from his farm.

WILL. Yes, if that is any business of yours.

JUDITH. Miles has been a model of rectitude in this village for many years.

WILL. A model of rectitude, eh? Perhaps that explains why he's a bankrupt.

BURBAGE. Will, try to be magnanimous in your older age, and not another Timon.

JUDITH. Another Timon!

BURBAGE. You don't remember Timon? *(quoting)* "I am Misanthropos, and hate mankind."

WILL. And who is there can love mankind?

JUDITH. Or womankind either?

WILL. Did not womankind beget the whole vile race? The wives cuckold their husbands, and decorate their heads with horns. The whores infect their customers, and festoon their flesh with sores.

JUDITH. So it is we women who are at fault.

WILL. All humankind is at fault.

JUDITH. Father, your face is dark, your eyes are hard. The last plays I saw of yours were about reconciliation, pity, and forgiveness. Can you not extend these feelings to your own family?

WILL. Forgive your mother her adultery with my brother?

BURBAGE. At least try to listen to her side of the story. You still have not produced any proof.

WILL. I have heard her side of the story –

JUDITH. Father!

BURBAGE. *(quoting)* "The quality of mercy is not strain'd."

(the voice of **ANNE** *as Portia)*

ANNE. "The quality of mercy is not strain'd.
It droppeth like the gentle rain from heaven
Upon the place beneath; it is twice blest;
It blesseth him that gives and him that takes."

WILL. *(dazed, hearing these lines from his own plays)* For your sake, Judith, I will restore Miles Chapman to his land. And for pity's sake, I will hear your mother's story one more time.

*(***JUDITH*** embraces him. ***WILL*** holds her at arm's length, looking into her eyes. Then releases her and walks into* **ANNE**'s *bedroom.)*

10. We have heard the chimes at midnight

(**SHAKESPEARE** *and* **BURBAGE** *at The Cage.*)

WILL. I have a confession, Dick

BURBAGE. Will?

WILL. The time passes so slowly.

BURBAGE. If you want the time to pass very slowly, just pretend you're watching one of Ben Jonson's Roman tragedies. It will add ten years to your life.

WILL. I admire Ben's classical work, dense though it is.

BURBAGE. I played the title role in *Sejanus: His Fall*, Will. I felt like a frog in a bowl of molasses.

WILL. I suspect you'll say the same about my work some day.

BURBAGE. That will I never, dear Will. Now that you've stopped writing I despair of ever finding such roles again. *(reciting)*
No more young Hamlet, old Hieronimo.
King Lear, the Grievéd Moor, and more beside
That lived in him have now for ever died.
Exit Burbage.

WILL. What's that?

BURBAGE. The epitaph I've written for myself.

WILL. Too long to fit on a headstone.

BURBAGE. *(disappointed)* Will.

WILL. I like the pun on "Grievéd Moor, and more beside." But why put Hieronimo on the same level as Hamlet, Lear and Othello?

BURBAGE. Be generous, Will, be generous. Will Shakespeare's melancholy Danish Prince would never have existed without Tom Kyd's lunatic Spanish Marshal, the first avenger.

WILL. You're right, Dick. I don't know myself any more.

BURBAGE. Put it down to the same bilious distemper that poisoned your relations with your daughter and your wife.

WILL. That cloud is lifting, Dick. But the one I trust the most is you. I will miss you sorely.

BURBAGE. And I will miss you, too, dear Will. Our debauches have been like disorderly sacraments, our carousals like rites of the damned. We have heard the chimes at midnight, have we not? We have heard them many times.

WILL. *(sadly)* That we have. That we have.

BURBAGE. And we will hear them soon again.

WILL. *(animated and merry for a moment)* Do you remember the time that voluptuous housewife invited you into her bed after a performance of *Richard III*, and you appeared, only to hear my voice behind her door, saying:

BURBAGE. "William the Conqueror has come before Richard III." Yes, but you always came before me. You were like a defective piece of field artillery.

WILL. And now, much more like a limp pistol.

BURBAGE. Well, go and find yourself some willing wench. Shouldn't be too hard to flush one out hereabouts.

WILL. My disease suppresses carnal appetite. And a good thing, too, since the affliction is infectious.

BURBAGE. Will, I do not wish to appear hardhearted, but I must leave you now. None of your problems are solvable by me, and I still have troubling issues of my own in London: refurbishing the rebuilt Globe, rounding up the actors who have scattered during the interregnum.

WILL. Good night, sweet Prince of players. Think of me when you are back in London scattering the roosters and inseminating the hens.

BURBAGE. Be resolute, Will. And firmly fix your quill in hand again.

WILL. And what ever would I do with it? My mind is as crippled as my fingers.

BURBAGE. At the least, make peace with your wife.

WILL. I'll think on it. But first, a tender and remorseful farewell to you.

(They embrace emotionally. **BURBAGE** *starts to leaves.* **WILL** *turns and speaks to him.)*

Father, do not leave before I have had the time to make a confession. I do not want to be a glover like you. I want to be an actor. I want to find my voice upon the stage, and spread your name across the land. Think upon it! An unknown boy from Stratford, with no more than a grammar school education, the idol of the London playhouses. Give me your blessing. Please.

*(***BURBAGE***, helping to relive this fantasy, puts his hand over* **WILL***'s head, and gives him his blessing.)*

9. Frailty thy name is woman

(**WILL** *in a room with* **ANNE.**)

WILL. Our marriage has never been a meeting of true minds. It was stopped up with impediments.

ANNE. The impediment was your absence.

WILL. No, the impediment was your dishonesty. All might have been different had you not tricked me into marriage.

ANNE. Marriage and procreation are the purpose of our sex.

WILL. Oh, and I thought it was deception.

ANNE. *(trying to cheer him)* Frailty, thy name is woman, eh?

WILL. Yes, so get thee to a nunnery.

ANNE. And get *thee* to a whorehouse. Appetite, thy name is man .

WILL. *(coming to himself)* Did I write that?

ANNE. No.

WILL. You know, you might have made a pretty good poet.

ANNE. I had no time for foolishness.

WILL. Appetite is the soul of man. Hum. You're saying that I alone was responsible for the incident in the rye field?

ANNE. It was a corn field.

WILL. The moon was cloud-blurred, the mist was thick. Neither of us was thinking clearly.

ANNE. My only memory of that event was of being repeatedly pricked – by burrs – breathless and panting after hot pursuit.

WILL. I was rather robust in those days, wasn't I. What else do you remember from that fateful night?

ANNE. I remember squeals of triumph from a conquering hero.

WILL. A conquering hero?

ANNE. How else would you describe yourself at that moment?

WILL. More like a goatish bumpkin.

ANNE. Who overcame a maiden's scruples…

WILL. *(skeptical)* A maiden?!! At twenty-six?!!

ANNE. …and got her with child.

WILL. And all these years I have believed… *(pause)*

ANNE. Yes?

WILL. …that the real conquest was yours. The temptor or the temptress, who sins most?

ANNE. Temptress! Was I that beguiling?

WILL. Beguiling enough to lure an innocent into a ryefield.

ANNE. For a night of plowing.

WILL. I was barely eighteen.

ANNE. And one of the few Stratford youths who had not yet been shipped off to the French wars.

WILL. Now I know why our marriage went so quickly sour. For you the only purpose of our pairing was breeding. I served no greater function than the Hathaway stud bull.

ANNE. All male animals serve that function in the end.

WILL. Producing progeny?

ANNE. While producing their own pleasure, as swiftly as possible.

WILL. Thank you for reminding me of my shortcomings.

ANNE. And thank you for reminding me of mine.

(They sit on the bed together.)

ANNE. Have none of your whores ever learned to wash a doublet? If you could manage to settle in one place for a moment, I would make you quite presentable again.

WILL. I thought I told you I am committed to staying in Stratford.

ANNE. Yes, but for how long?

WILL. For good and all.

*(**ANNE** touches him, then kisses him.)*

WILL. Now that is the Anne Hathaway that lured me into that cornfield.

ANNE. Well, at least you remember the place correctly.

WILL. I remember more than the place.

ANNE. *(tenderly)* Will!

(She tries to pull him down on the bed.)

WILL. *(removing her arms from his neck)* I can't.

ANNE. What is the matter?

WILL. I can't.

(He exits.)

(lights down)

11. I did her wrong

(WILL *comes into* ANNE*'s room.* JUDITH *is sitting with her on the bed, knitting.*)

WILL. My last remaining brother, Richard, is dead.

ANNE. Do not say that!

WILL. I have just come from the infirmary.

JUDITH. You saw my uncle dead.

WILL. Yes, my dear Perdita.

JUDITH. I am Judith, Father.

WILL. My daughter Perdita, who was lost to me and now is found.

JUDITH. Your daughter Judith, Father, who never left your side.

WILL. Pray, do not mock me. I am a foolish fond old man.

ANNE. Will, stop this nonsense. You are frightening me.

WILL. Hold me. I am not certain who I am.

ANNE. *(holding him)* You are William Shakespeare of Stratford-Upon-Avon. The premiere playwright of England.

WILL. Where have I been?

ANNE. You were with Richard.

WILL. Richard? Yes, Richard. I watched him die. And with his last breath…

ANNE. Yes?

WILL. He begged of me his pardon.

ANNE. For what?

WILL. *(difficult for him to say)* For defaming Desdemona's character.

ANNE. Are you confusing Richard with your dead brother, Gilbert?

WILL. Gilbert is dead?

JUDITH. Father, try to hold a thought. You told us Gilbert was in love with mother, which made you doubt Hamnet's paternity and mine.

WILL. Richard swore that was a lie, that Gilbert never touched your mother.

JUDITH. You should never have doubted her.

WILL. I saw them paddling palms and pinching fingers. I'd always thought Mamilius was my blood, his nose the perfect picture of my own.

JUDITH. *(to* **ANNE***)* Is he talking about Hamnet?

WILL. But my jealous nature was his murderer. My poor dead child, who died after I had falsely charged Hermione with adultery. *(hitting himself on the head with his hand)* Fool! Fool! Credulous, disingenuous fool. How could I believe her false? I! Who have always known the only certainty was doubt. Woe, you gullible fool.

ANNE. Will, stop this.

JUDITH. Father. *(both are holding* **WILL** *tightly)*

WILL. I have done you wrong. I have done you wrong. But it is reparable. I can change my will and restore you both to your rightful estates. The lioness share for you, dear Gertrude. And for Ophelia, her full marriage portion.

ANNE. You will never write another will.

WILL. Can you forgive me? Hermione forgave me. Cordelia forgave me. "No cause," she said, "no cause."

ANNE. I am Anne, your wife, Will. And this is Judith, your daughter.

WILL. They were all my wives, all my daughters, and I have wronged them all. *(to* **ANNE***)* I have abused you, Desdemona, with my vile suspicions. I have abused you, Hermione, with my baseless jealousy. I have abused you, Ophelia, with my brutish insults. I have abused you, Imogen, with my inordinate pride. *(to* **JUDITH***)* And I have been a thankless father to my Cordelia, my Marina, my Miranda, my Perdita. Daughters and wives. I have wronged you all. Pray, do not blame me for my blindness.

ANNE. No blame, no blame.

WILL. And will you hold me once again? *(They embrace.)* It is a comfort to feel welcome in your good warm arms.

ANNE. And in your good warm bed.

WILL. My best bed. My second best bed. My funeral pyre.

ANNE. *(alarmed)* Will.

WILL. Strike up the drum towards Troy. The Greeks are defiling Cressida. Helen is cuckolding Menelaus. Andromache will assume her widow's weeds after Achilles drags her slaughtered husband Hector through the city streets. Lechery, lechery, still wars and lechery.

JUDITH. Alas, he's mad.

(They gather around him.)

WILL. Fix my quill in my hand. I must change my will.

*(As **JUDITH** works to put **SHAKESPEARE**'s quill in his gnarled hand, the lights come up on Lawyer **COLLINS** and **SUSANNA**, and all of them are back in **COLLIN**'s office.)*

12. I am dying, Egypt

COLLINS. Say Master Shakespeare, how may I be of service to you?

(WILL *is sitting silent, on a couch, quill stuck stiffly in his hand, staring straight in front of him at some unseen object. He then begins murmuring to himself in an unknown tongue.*)

COLLINS. Master Shakespeare? Master Shakespeare? Can you inform me of what you wish me to do?

ANNE. Give him a moment. He has been much distracted lately.

SUSANNA. For very cogent reasons, as I hear of it.

JUDITH. What are you speaking of?

SUSANNA. Our mother's misconduct.

ANNE. Susanna, stop your priggish moralizing.

JUDITH. You are not in the strongest position to question another woman's morality.

SUSANNA. I was fully exonerated by a duly constituted court.

JUDITH. You were exonerated by falsely purchased testimony. And, as I am beginning to understand, with the expert help of an infatuated lawyer.

ANNE. This wrangling is most unseemly when your father is so ill.

COLLINS. I agree. Master Shakespeare, I have a full agenda this morning. Why have you come to see me?

(**SHAKESPEARE** *continues to stare into space, mumbling.*)

COLLINS. I would guess it has something to do with your will. Do you wish to amend it?

SUSANNA. Francis!

(*more silence*)

SUSANNA. He is clearly in no condition to change his will again. His mind is gone.

(**SHAKESPEARE** *continues to stare ahead in front of him.*)

ANNE. Come Judith. Come Will. Let us leave this place.

(*They proceed to gather their things, when* **WILL** *suddenly begins to speak.*)

WILL. The sea, all water, yet receives rain still,
And in abundance addeth to his store:
So shalt thou being rich in Will add to thy Will
One will of mine to make thy large Will more.

SUSANNA. Still harping on his will.

JUDITH. No, he is quoting from one of his sonnets.

(*She goes to his side.*)

WILL. *(to* **ANNE***)* I will never again entertain a clear conscience. Please forgive me.

SUSANNA. Oh, these endless expressions of guilt. Show true repentance and God will forgive you.

WILL. Spiteful Goneril, here is my curse on you.
If you must teem,
Create your child of spleen; that it may live,
And be a thwart disnatured torment to you!...
How sharper than a serpent's tooth it is
To have a thankless child!

SUSANNA. *(deeply wounded)* That is a perfectly dreadful thing to say to a daughter.

JUDITH. Do not excite yourself. Be at peace, Father.

WILL. *(to* **JUDITH***)* You do me wrong to take me out o' the grave:
Thou art a soul in bliss; but I am bound
Upon a wheel of fire, that mine own tears
Do scald like molten lead.

JUDITH. He takes me for Cordelia.

WILL. *(to* **JUDITH***)* And my poor fool is hang'd! No, no, no life!

Why should a dog, a horse, a rat, have life,

And thou no breath at all? Thou'lt come no more,

Never, never, never, never, never!

Pray you, undo this button:

JUDITH. Father, I am alive and by your side.

WILL. The miserable change now at my end

Lament nor sorrow at; but please your thoughts

In feeding them with those my former fortunes

Wherein I lived, the greatest prince o' the world,

The noblest; Now my spirit is going;

I can no more.

COLLINS. The playwright is burying himself in his own plays.

(to **ANNE***)*

WILL. I am dying, Egypt, dying; only

I here importune death awhile, until

Of many thousand kisses the poor last

I lay upon thy lips. The potent poison

Quite oer-crows my spirit.

(He goes to kiss her, but stumbles and stops. His eyes glaze. He goes silent again, mumbling to himself. Then he sits perfectly still. Slowly and ceremoniously, Lawyer **COLLINS** *removes the quill from his crab-like grip, as* **ANNE** *begins to weep at his feet and* **JUDITH** *holds him tightly.)*

COLLINS. There will be no further will. *(He breaks the quill in two.)*

SUSANNA. *(triumphantly)* And no alteration in my inheritance.

JUDITH. Your inheritance. Your inheritance. As if our father's only legacy was the furniture he left to you.

ANNE. Farms and fourposters. Chattels and tenancies. Those were not the birthright of this unhappy man.

(**BURBAGE** *bursts on stage holding a sheaf of papers.*)

BURBAGE. Will, they told me you'd be here. Great news! A pair of London publishers are putting out ten of your plays. Here are the leaves. And your fellow actors, Heminge and Condell, intend to include all thirty-six in a massive Folio.

(**WILL** *is immobile, his eyes unmoving.*)

Will, do you hear? We need your approval before we proceed with the printing. All you have to do is sign the title page. Where's your quill?

(**WILL** *rises to his feet, standing straight and resolute.*)

WILL. I'll drown my book. *(He suddenly pitches forward, but remains supported by his wife and daughter.)*

BURBAGE. What's the matter with him?

COLLINS. He has fallen from delusion into darkness.

BURBAGE. Is he – ?

COLLINS. His body lives. His mind is gone.

ANNE. Gone. Gone. My amorous stripling of the cornfield.

JUDITH. Gone, gone. My tender sailor of the paper boats.

SUSANNA. Gone? Gone? When was he not gone, this delinquent truant, this selfish man? But his last will left his legacy to me.

BURBAGE. No, his legacy was bequeathéd to us all.

(**COLLINS** *takes his place by* **SUSANNA**'*s side.* **BURBAGE** *and the two weeping women collect around the inert* **SHAKESPEARE.** **SUSANNA** *remains absorbed in her scanning of the will. After a moment,* **BURBAGE** *turns to the audience, and repeats:)*

BURBAGE. His legacy was bequeathéd to us all. A birthright whose beneficiaries are as numberless as the stars.

(He kisses the pages in his hand, then strews them into the auditorium as if they were goodbye gifts to the audience. A lingering light is left on **WILL**'s *face, then dims.)*

End of Play